# Dedication

To Matthew, Bradley, Sarah and Pierce, with all my love,

Grandma Lois

# The Friendly Visit

One fine day, a funny frog named Frankie hopped down the sidewalk on his way to visit his friend Silly Mickey the Monkey who lived in the treehouse at the park. Because they were the best of friends, they decided to go to the zoo together to see Larry the Leopard and Benny the Bear who happened to be sitting in the sun when they arrived.

"What are you doing?" Frankie asked them.

Larry and Benny said that they were thinking about visiting their friends Morris the Big Moose and Little Denny the Deer who lived in the big field at the end of the zoo.

"Let's surprise Morris and Denny," Larry and Benny said.

So off they went—Frankie, Silly Mickey, Larry, and Benny—together. On the way, they had some fun. They hopped, galloped, jumped, did flip flops, and did somersaults. They laughed, roared and waved to the people who watched them.

Then they saw Morris and Denny who were having a picnic with their friend, Blackie the Green-Eyed Cat.

"Come join us," they said.

So, Frankie, Silly Mickey, Larry, and Benny joined up with Morris, Denny and Blackie. They all had a happy, fun time eating, playing, sharing, being together, acting silly, and being funny in the field. It was a beautiful sunny day and the birds were singing.

Then they all said, "This is the best play time in the whole world. Let's do this lots of times."

Then they all hugged, shared big high-fives, and went back home.

# A Silly Walk

One day, a funny man and his friend went for a walk. Along the way, they met a friendly dinosaur who was busy cooking and eating a delicious hot dog. After a bit of time, they saw a gigantic man who was holding a tiny boy in his hand. So, they all decided to be friends and go for a silly walk down the road together. They were something else—rambling along, happy, and singing together. Then they met a funny car that was chugging on and beeping its horn to try to pass them. Suddenly, the car stopped, and who do you think got out?

It was Dipsy, Laa-Laa, Po, Tinky Winky and Barney!

How exciting it was. And who did they all see next? It was Winnie the Pooh!

"Hey, you guys, come with me, it's almost time for Halloween. Follow me." Pooh said.

They all went to many houses, but guess what? There were no people there—none at all! So, they continued their silly walk, singing and laughing together and did not stop until they saw the Halloween man.

"Hi, Guys," he said. "You're too early. We still have to get ready. We have to get decorated and have to put our trick or treat costumes on."

Off they all went with Winnie the Pooh in the lead and Barney, Tinky Winky, Po, Laa-Laa, Dipsy and all the others singing loud and clear...

"WE'LL BE BACK ON HALLOWEEN. You better be ready for us then!"

# A Special Story

The doggy said, "woof, woof" as she ran across the field.

The cows were there too. They said, "moo, moo."

And there was Daddy Jon sitting on the big red tractor. The sun was shining on this very special day in Wellesport, U.S.A. Even the sheep were "baa-baaing," and the piggies were squealing with delight, "oink, oink!"

"What is happening?" asked Frankie the Frog as he jumped over a bed of stones to meet his new friend Stanley the Sneaky Snake who was squiggling up the path.

"I don't really know," said Kitty the Cat who was walking her kittens over the grassy way.

"Meow, meow, what a day!"

Timmy the Sleepy Turtle came out from hiding under his shell and smiled at the whole parade of animals now meeting together in front of his eyes.

"Timmy! You don't want to miss this special day," the whole group said. "Stay awake and don't go back to sleep! Stay alert today!"

Up in the tree, birds were singing and chirping, and a silly squirrel ran over the branches of the tree and did a fancy kind of dance.

"Today! Today! I will do my dance today! What is today? What is today?"

There was something going on! How exciting! But what? They all wanted to jump with joy! But why? Well, let us see!

Near the barn you could hear the horse gleefully saying, "neigh, neigh." The horse was named Hermy and he was bending down to whisper to the family of chickens coming across the yard to greet him. "Can you feel the joy, Mrs. Chicken?" asked Hermy. "Are you and your chickies ready for this day? What a day today! What fun it will be!"

Inside the farmhouse there was the aroma of a baking cake and excitement all around. The little girl was playing happily with her new dollhouse filled with furniture and special people. The baby boy was laughing and keeping happy sitting on the floor with all his trucks, toys, animals and books. What a day today, of course, of course. A special day!

Momma Emma was busy getting ready for the day. There were balloons to fill, decorations to set, food to get ready, and sweets to get out. The people will come today, this day! We don't have to wait anymore, anymore! Hooray!

Momma Emma saw Daddy Jon through the window. He was home from the field and had put the big red tractor back into the big red barn.

"Come get ready!" she called. "The cake will soon be done! It is time for fun. Look at the table, the presents! Everything is almost done, and the cake smells yummy!"

The doggy barked once, of course. "Woof." She is so smart. Time to get dressed for the party! For who? Oh! You know, don't you? Sally, the big sister, is as pretty as can be in a pink flowered dress, and her hair is flowing with bunches of curls. A big smile is there, too. She knows the joy! For who? For who? Here come the people. The children! The mommies and daddies, the grandmas and poppas, and all those who love. For who today? There is Kitty with her babies, "meow, meow," and doggy, "woof, woof," the piggies, "oink, oink," and the sheep "baa, baa."

There is Hermy the Horse again, neighing with glee and Frankie the Frog and Stanley the squiggly snake. The cows are mooing so loudly! Oh! We forgot the goats, "maa-maaaing," and the ducks "quack, quacking"... and who else? Timmy the Turtle is awake, the birdies are chirping, and the chickens are saying, "cluck, cluck," while the squirrel in the tree is dancing away. For who today? Let me tell you for who! For who!

It's for a darling little boy with a beautiful face and happy smile who looks and sees and wonders what this can be.

"For me?" Of course! For you this day! Blow your candles out little one! Eat your cake and open your presents. We have waited for this day! We all love you on this, your special day!

Happy Birthday, little Peter! And many, many more to come. And from all, please let us say with all the joy that we feel:

HAPPY BIRTHDAY PRECIOUS ONE! HAPPY BIRTHDAY TO YOU!

# A Day with David

One warm summer day, out of the blue water by the seashore, walked a tiny, tiny crab. This was the first adventure for our little friend from the sea.

Where to go and what to do and all that sand and stuff to explore—wow! And meeting those big tall people's feet that get in your way, and their LOUD voices when they realize you are underfoot. YOWIE!

Here I go. Tramp, tramp, tramp. Walk, walk, walk. I'm so busy. I never saw so many people in all my life.

Oh—there is some food! A young boy threw a crust of bread to me from  his sandwich. What a nice guy he is. Yummy. PB and J. I heard they all like that *com-bin-a-tion*—my first big word!

I hear him being called. Jackson! That's a nice name. He noticed me and then runs to fill his pail with cold water—and—the next thing I know, I'm swimming in it. My new friend?

"He's sort of a cute guy," they say.

Who are they talking about? Me or Jackson? I guess it's me. Now I'm a celebrity.

If I'm so famous, I need a name. What will that be? What do I hear?

"David."

Where in the world did he come up with that one?

David it is. Here we go. Back to the beach house to get out of the sun and clean up.

Me or them?

Let me loose to go back to my adventure walk. Please, No way Jose!

Tramp, Tramp, Tramp. Here we are at Grandpa's Place. First things first as I sit alone in the pail. Here comes Jackson back.

"Hi Crabby David," I hear. "Time for your supper." I'm thrown a few pellets from the last crab's food. Yummy. What next. I'm being covered up so I can't get out, but they don't know my talents. I'm strong, and when no one is looking, I ESCAPE and start my travels. I end up in someone's bedroom in their comfy bed where I wait...

Great Aunt Lily is preparing for bed and I hear the ruckus about where I went off to. Probably in the woods and gone?

Well, get into bed, lady and we'll see. Barely a second goes by when she rests her head down, and then I make a move. Nice hair lady—just been washed and a nice shampoo smell. I start my approach on the pillow from underneath...

The loudest scream in the whole world is what I hear, and then I laugh and laugh to myself, "Never fear, David is here!"

And remember kids, watch out for us little crabs, we can really get into your hair. And we're smarter than you think.

Ha, Ha, Ha!

# Tabbles and Glory

Cousins—that is what they are, yet they are so very different. Not the same at all. They don't see each other often because they live far apart, a long, long way away.

Tabbles came to be on a bright, brisk day as the wind was blowing and the sun was warming her fuzzy face. She simply decided that it was the right time to make herself some new friends and maybe find a cozy place to live, eat and do what she loves to do best—sleep in the sun and be happy!

You see, Tabbles, at the time, was small and being the little kitten that she was, knew that it was very important to seek and find an especially nice family to live with who would love and take care of her.

The Poseyfields lived in a big house surrounded by lots of trees, and when Tabbles took a little walk, it was this house that came into view. Her heart said yes, and that was how it all started.

Mr. Poseyfield was fixing his lawnmower near the garage when he felt something at his foot. Looking down, he saw this tiny little face looking up at him and saying, "Hi, there!"

Well, not really, but probably!

He called to his wife, Betsy, who was baking three apple pies in the kitchen while the children were napping and said, "Come see our little visitor and bring a little bowl of milk."

Now Betsy Poseyfield was thinking, "What's he up to now? I'll never finish my pies and the boys will be up romping around in no time!" Taking the bowl of milk, she went to the garage—and there was Tabbles!

"Where in the world did she come from?"

Moe Poseyfield scratched his head and said, "Sure don't know."

At about the same time, Glory was about to join the Poseyfield's relatives. They were looking for a tiny, special puppy. It would take a little time before the cousins would meet and get to know each other. Now you know the secret of Glory!

Tabbles settled in with the Poseyfields and the little boys, Micky and Bobby, had a new toy. The name Tabbles came to be because little Bobby couldn't say "apples" as a name and it came out as "Tabbles!" Micky, at the time, decided to let Tabbles sleep in his tee-pee and when the kitten was out of sight, everyone knew she was in her "tee."

One day, when no one was looking, Tabbles found a new bed. Guess where! After spending a lot of time searching the whole house, they found her under the chair in the family room sleeping very peacefully.

Tabbles had just begun to be! But what is next? To grow! She grew and learned to do the usual things like jumping and scratching and racing around crazy! One day, Betsy found Tabbles on the kitchen counter asleep after finishing some milk left in a bowl. She had been napping near the window as the sun shown through. The warmth had lulled her to sleep. My home, she thought. My home. But, where was Glory?

The Poseyfields' relatives, Jack and Emma Dillon, after searching on the internet, yelled, "Bingo!" And the next week, brought home a very little puppy

who came to be the glory of their lives. And this was how "Glory" came to be! Glory simply took over the household and to be precise, made herself a home! She loved her bed, she loved attention, and she loved to sharpen her puppy teeth on the kitchen cabinets. And when she was scolded, she always looked up with the most adorable puppy eyes. It's OK, Glory thought, cause Gramma Dora would come to visit, and she made it alright again.

One day after Glory got bigger and Gramma Dora came, Glory jumped up and gave her a hug with her paws—and that's the truth! Thank you, Gramma!

Glory went everywhere and did everything with Jack and Emma. One day, they all took a long ride in the car, and when they got where they were going, they arrived at the Poseyfields. The cousins were about to meet! Tabbles and Glory! And what a meeting it was!

It began with a sniff of noses, a quiet look, and then "the chase"!

Never again would life be the same! Hissing, barking and running all over the house, up and down the stairs, and all around! The cousins had met, eye to eye, look to look, and the challenge and dilemma to figure out who was in charge began! Mickey and Bobby were delighted! What fun! The visits to see each other were not very often, and in two years' time, the boys, Micky and Bobby, had two new cousins themselves. Sally and Petey came along to complete a family for Jack and Emma. Glory felt lost at times, but she loved the children and she was so good with them. She watched over them like a nanny and always made sure they were doing OK.

Now, when Tabbles and Glory got to see each other, they no longer hissed and chased and barked. They were like two, old contented friends who shared a loving family. One night, Moe Poseyfield found the two of them snuggled together on... would you believe, the big chair? The big, comfortable chair was Tabbles' special sleeping nook! And hers alone!

Isn't it true how wonderful and good it feels to belong to a warm and happy home? Tabbles made the right choice when she saw that big house belonging to all the Poseyfields, and so did Jack and Emma when they picked out their special Glory. A love prevailed, and children came, too. And now when all the "cousins" meet, it is such an exciting and busy time! I wonder what Tabbles and Glory are thinking?

I BET YOU KNOW!

# Reginald Robot

Reginald Robot was in trouble and he didn't like the feeling at all. The problem was this, simply stated: for once in his life he didn't have anything to do. There was no work, no cooking, no cleaning, no lifting, no moving, no driving, not even ten white shirts to iron. He was in quite a dither and was not a "happy camper" to say the least. Now, what on Earth could be the thing that got him into this dilemma anyhow?

It was the year 2050. Yesterday was an Indian summer day in October, and his favorite people to work for, Hector and

Harriet Doolittle, (Reggie always liked their last name because it was SO right! Didn't he do all the work?) had left for a six-month Safari to Africa. They were not coming home until they found a perfect elephant family to bring back with them. Reggie was thinking they would need more than a robot to move those lazy elephants, especially if they were downright grouchy ones! Oh well, not to wonder about this now... Reggie had to get busy and quickly!

He turned on his new IBM, no-key, do-everything, talk-to-computer, gave his password with a funny smile, and began his surf to adventure! Reggie relaxed and tried a lot of maneuvers until he found himself in a "chat" with the top specialist at the Rockville, Rhode Island Center for Collectors of Precious Stones, Pebbles, Gravel and Gigantic Rocks. They were in a dither there too, and Professor TibbIe needed lots of help—and quickly!

Cornelius Tibble, or as he was more commonly called, Corny, was so excited when Reggie told him he needed work to keep him busy and moving that he almost fell off the old La-Z-Boy recliner chair that he was sitting on in his office. "Reggie, I have a six-month time period to bring us back to a normal state here at the Center," Corny said.

"What can I do for you Corny?" Reggie asked.

Reggie felt just a wee bit elated himself. "Well, Reggie" said Corny, "the problem is that the entire collection here has turned  a funny color of orange and we don't know what has made this happen. It's been slowly taking on this color for the past three weeks and now we look like a pumpkin patch ready for Halloween! I'm as grumpy as a goblin and without energy to boot!"

"I'll be up there in no time" said Reggie. "I just have to pack a few things, leave the dog at the vet, e-mail the Doolittles, and close up the mansion—pronto, on the double and all that jazz—and I'll be off and running to you!"

The trip to Rhode Island took longer than expected because Reggie needed new glasses. He had  to take time to be tested so that his vision would be superb when his new job began. The eyes of robots have to be perfect-plus! Nothing can get in their way!

Looking powerfully better, Reggie was on his way! There would be no stops except at a new McDonald's on the highway. They're serving Chinese food there now, and Reggie likes their yummy French fries in lobster sauce. (The Robotmobile also needed a drive-through wash.) And then he was on his way!

 Reggie arrived in Rockville, Rhode Island as the sun was setting, and Corny Tibble greeted him with open arms. They took time to get acquainted, realizing that they had gone to the same

movie and helped each other figure out  the ending which was very strange. Reggie was to sleep at the new hotel next to the Center where he was to work. All well and good and content to have him there, Corny brought iced tea and cookies for them while he told the story of the color orange ... weird and stranger than the ending of the movie. The new friends began their task of outlining their strategy to correct the damage to the inventory at the Center. Corny then left and Reggie crawled into bed, tired after his long and exciting day.

In the morning, Corny showed Reggie through the entire  Center, and after the lengthy walk-through, it became evident to Reggie just how weird and peculiar the actual problem seemed to be. Seeing orange through the window on a bright sunny day was glaring, and Reggie was glad he had paid extra for a good pair of sunglasses. He needed them right about now. The two friends were in agreement—finding the answer surely would take time and something called "Patience Plus!"

As it was a Sunday, there were no other workers there, and Corny and Reggie banged heads together, so to speak, and came up with nothing except that there also seemed to be a slight aroma throughout the place. Reggie laughed when he said, "It's a smell like... ha, ha, ha... an orange, Corny! It really is!" Reggie muffled his laugh when he saw the hurt look on Corny's face. "Sorry Corny. I'm beat. Let's call it a day."

Reggie went back to the Hi-Tech Hotel and ordered a nice steak potato pie for dinner and then relaxed and watched old movies on the Disney Channel. He knew he would be a busy-bee soon!

Reggie ate a big breakfast the next morning, did his exercise routine, took his Everything Vitamin (which was in the shape of a bagel) and rumbled across to the Center to begin his new work.

The days flew by and still no clue could be found to explain the orange on the rocks. They tried everything to get rid of the color! They tried washing, steaming, freezing, solutions, chemicals, deodorizers, and then  rubbing and polishing! Nothing helped! The aroma now was strongly citrus and yukky too! To make things worse, Reggie heard from the Doolittles. Hector said Harriet was lonesome for her home and her puppy, Little One the St. Bernard, and wanted to come back soon. No elephants had been gotten yet, either.

Reggie had to act quickly... and fast too!

Cornelius Tibble and his work crew appreciated all Reggie's help and ideas. On November 30th, they had a surprise birthday party for Reggie. The cake was delicious even though it was a carrot one and it had a big frosted orange carrot on top!

Reggie was a good sport, even when they presented him with an orangey t-shirt—XXX large, too!

About two weeks later, while trying a new theory using a technique with the air circulating system, Reggie saw light bulbs going off in his robot thought mechanism device! He felt he was beginning to get a long-awaited clue. And the idea was ripe as—would you believe -- an orange! He thought, "we're on our way to a solution to this mess!"

Reggie and Corny were excited! Somehow and from somewhere, there was a finely filtered orange substance seeping through the system and depositing itself on the rocks and everything, and attaching the substance to them. What is causing this and how to remove the culprit and leave these precious stones looking right again? Was this the answer?

That night, while Reggie was eating a delicious casserole of chicken and asparagus topped with a pumpkin sauce at the hotel, he asked his waiter when the hotel had opened. The waiter  then told him that the grand opening had been shortly before Reggie arrived. They were late opening because they had to repair their air-circulating system which was found to be not working properly! Reggie almost choked on his food! Ah ha! The waiter then informed him that a specialist in this area had to be called in to fix the problem. The waiter said that it took a couple of weeks, but now everything was working well. Reggie thanked the waiter and slowly finished his dessert of apple ice cream with whipped cream.

Reggie did not sleep that night at all. There was a connection to the Center problem, that's for sure, but how, what and why was it happening?

To be sure Reggie was the first one at breakfast the next morning and was greeted with a large glass of freshly squeezed orange juice, no pulp, just as he always liked it. He was very thirsty.

Reggie stopped to see the manager of the hotel after breakfast, and Mr. Bramble had no clue as to what the answer could be when he heard the story. But he did say that all the systems operated from an area off their kitchen, and there was a special disposal system for the Florida orange rinds they used after squeezing. The customers paid extra to taste their wonderful juice. Reggie was thinking of a big charge on his bill because he was an OJ lover too! Reggie asked Mr. Bramble to get Corny here on the double. A search had to begin immediately!

The entire crew of workers started the search with Reggie Robot on top of it all. Reggie's brain was working swiftly and thought, "we'll get this finished in no time and I'll be home for the holidays for sure! And in two months, not six, because I have to get the mansion ready for the Doolittles!"

Suddenly, Sydney the crew leader shouted, "What have we here?" Everyone rushed to his side. "We have a small crack on the side of the orange disposal mechanism and something seems to be seeping into a misplaced filter in the air circulating system close by. The Center's system has to be connected somehow!" They knew before any repair was to be done, an antidote had to be flushed through the disposal system to clean the stones  and rocks. Sydney had heard of something like this happening in Pokemon, California, and he called them immediately.

After waiting to get through, an answer came across the computer screen. "This is what you have to do. Take a mixture of water, baking soda and diluted tea in equal parts and slowly let that wash through the systems for a couple of days, then you'll be back to normal in no time!" Simple. They had to give it a try!

In what seemed like two years instead of two days, the process continued back at the Center. The beautiful rocks, stones, gravel and pebbles were slowly returning to their normal colors. The citrus aroma had changed to the cleanest smell Corny's nose had ever inhaled!

All repairs were done, and Reggie's work was completed. He got a big high-five and a hug from Corny and then packed the Robotmobile with a cooler full of the best pulp-free orange juice he had ever tasted! He put on his sunglasses and his new soccer cap (a gift from everyone) and drove away. Reggie was on his way back to his job at the Doolittles and the elephants were on their way too! He smiled to himself and thought, "what did they give me a soccer cap for anyhow? I've never even played soccer!"

# Lailah the Lighthouse

Here I am shining my light brightly on this warm evening. The first flowers of spring are pushing their way upward from the beds that surround me all around this island near the sea.

I have been here for a very long time and have shone my light to many boats who have needed me to guide their way—so many times. It's my job, a good job, and I've been here, and

I have been happy. Now you ask, how can a lighthouse be happy? Well, I'm going to tell you! So, sit back and listen, and when I'm finished, I know you will then realize what being happy is all about.

The people who gave thought to me and saw my need to help the many boats and vessels travelling the sea, lived many years ago. There was a man named James and he had a son, Douglas. Little as he was called at the time, the boy followed his father everywhere. Douglas liked to watch as Dad spent long hours at his boat building work—this was how money was made back then to live, buy food, clothes and all the other necessary things.

One day, James stood back and scratched his head and said to Douglas, "Little One, someday we will build something together... think. Think and we will make a dream come true."

Douglas, even as little as he was, always listened to his father, and so it came to be. One day, some years later, the boy was walking and holding a lantern light to guide their way home as he and his father brought firewood to the house to use in the fireplace to warm the family on a cold winter night. The sea winds were blowing, and in the distance, you could hear the boats and their fog horns. "Help" it sounded like—"help our way."

"Papa," Douglas quickly said, "we have to light their way. We have to build a big light for the vessels and make it tall and high. And we can all live in this house and be happy and proud and helpful. Please, Papa, let us do this together."

And so, as the thawing of Spring began, and the ground and soil became warmer, the building of Douglas' dream took hold. It sat on top of a hill looking out at the sea beneath. Slowly the house of light took shape, and the new construction brought people from all around to see the special new house that would be like a shining star. What a great idea! How wonderful! Who thought of it? There were many questions and praise for this work being done.

Douglas was so happy, and James stood proud not only looking at the lighthouse, but also at his son who was also happy, happy.

When the time came to finish their work and move into the house to work the light, Douglas jumped with happy thoughts. My lighthouse must have a name. A very special name. What can we name her? What? What?

Douglas wanted a different name for this light that was to be a beacon of hope for boats afloat, but what kind of name could you call a lighthouse?

One day, Douglas' little baby sister was toddling around the grass near the light. Their mother was walking closely behind. Douglas loved to hug his little sister, and as she came running to him, he caught her in a big hug and said, "Annie, what can we call the lighthouse?"

As Annie was still trying to form her words to talk, she got so excited and happily cried out in joy to her brother—" Lailah, Lailah"—trying to say lighthouse, but it was all she could say.

And that is how on a warm day, and as the sun was shining on the sea beneath, a little girl and her brother found a precious, happy-sounding name for their lighthouse now complete.

Through the years, there were many lighthouse keepers and families caring for this light of lights. And all found a happy home here and fell in love with their happy life doing a special job.

Now, today it is simpler to light the light. A lighthouse keeper is not really needed as much anymore because there is such a thing known as *automation* done without the need of a keeper's hand. It's probably done now with a computer to make the light do its work. So, why am I happy? Don't you know now?

Put yourself on a grassy hill surrounded by flowers with the sea beneath. Add children smiling, happiness abounding, people visiting, laughter all around, happy faces, and summer fun, even on a snowy winter or rainy foggy day. I am here, warmed by a fireplace and cuddling children through the years. I remain tall and safe, keeping safe the sailors of the sea. And I smile.

What a pretty name for a lighthouse. I am Lailah—a shining ray of happiness. And I think back to that little girl many years past. I see her still running to hug her brother. And I realize—If you can make someone else's life brighter, your work is well done!

Isn't that right!

# Did you have a good day?

# Acknowledgement

Thank you to all my family who listened to my stories as they were written and supported me with my endeavor.

To Sarah Franco—a creative writing instructor who read my stories and encouraged me to publish.

To my dear friend and typist Melanie Racioppi who also was my real estate sale as a Realtor™ and to all those who were the stories and people my book came to be about—the wonderful entire loving people in my life.

# About the Author

 Lois Rosenfield is a retired registered nurse and Realtor™. She has lived in Rhode Island since 1962, is the mother of two children and has four grandchildren. She has been married to her husband David for 62 years.

Happy Times is her first book.

Made in the USA
Columbia, SC
16 October 2018